My Name is Ciji

The Ciji Book Series

A novel by
Lettie Lawman

To order additional copies of this book, contact:
Bookwhip
1-855-339-3589
www.bookwhip.com

Chapter 1

School? A total waste of time. This was my grandfather's opinion, of course. Growing up among five siblings made it very difficult to spend time alone. My younger sisters kept trying to show me a new thing she had learned or found. My older brothers tried too hard to entice me to play with them—almost all the time. My mother always encouraged me to play with my younger sisters. "Obi, you need to show her that you care," she would always say in her candid manner. I could not fathom her reason for making those dismal statements.

I would reply, "I think I already did." I spent so much time with my siblings that I jumped at every chance to be by myself. This is when spending weekends and holidays with my grandparents came in handy. Spending weekends with my grandparents akin to having time away from my siblings and almost like being by myself. I yearn spending time alone.

By the time I was almost nine, my grandparents knew how much I enjoyed being alone so whenever my father dropped me off, they let me decide how to spend the time. My grandparents also, on the other hand, tried to nurture my sibling spirit through gaudy encouragement.

My grandmother showed me my father's room where he had grow up and said, "You can always stay here, Obi. It used to be your father's." I looked around in utmost wonder at my father's prior abode.

And I said, "Cool." So I even had my own room in my grandparents' house. The room was my heaven—quiet, small, and cozy. There were some very old toys I was intrigued by. Yes, they said I could play with these toys: toy carriages, toy soldiers, toy animals, all wooden and downright old. Some of these toy carriages had detached wheels but I still liked them as they were. I could also sit quietly and read some books that I would bring in.

From the window, I could see a narrow dirt path. Once in a while, I could hear footsteps of people passing by with clay pots in their hands. They later passed through again with the pots on their heads. Sometimes they were accompanied by children who would first walk by in dry clothes and later would be in wet clothes. So I started to think that my grandparents lived near a stream. It was noteworthy that people trickled by this house all day long but as an astute reader, I read my books.

One day my grandfather brought me into his room and said, "Now, let's test this rumor about school." I looked at him with incredulous eyes remembering that I aspired to be like him, still he was hospitable, I thought.

I looked at him and said, "Rumors about school?" He nodded. I was going to ask what he meant, but before I could say anything further he picked up a small bottle from his table, opened it, and handed me a pill from it. I held the tablet in my hand with uncertainty, wary about what this could be all about. My head started swimming with all kinds of murky thoughts.

"Tell me the name of that medicine," he said motioning to the pill. I turned it to the other side, but there was nothing written on it. "They teach you to read in school. So tell me the name of the pill in your hand," he prodded.

I said, "Grandpa, there is nothing written on this pill. All I can say is that it is white." He took the pill from me, put it back in the bottle, and led me to the parlor. Dede, as we fondly called my grandpa continued to shake his head with the same momentum as we went into the radiant parlor. He seemed be in total disbelief.

We sat down, and he said, "I told your dad that school is a waste of time and money, and I still think so, even more strongly now than before. I don't know why he won't send you to learn a trade. You know, something you can do with your hands."

Then he went on to give me a list of things people could do with their hands. He mentioned blacksmiths, pestle makers, paddle makers, and even canoe makers. I looked at my grandfather and thought that he must not have been educated; otherwise, he would have known that the pill had nothing written on it. There was no way I could have known the name of this medicine unless it was written on it. I still saw my grandfather as someone that knows a whole lot of things in spite of this incident. How else could you explain the fact that people came to him for answers to their puzzling questions? How was it that he was a chief in my village? What about the stories he told of things that happened long ago and he was able to remember them all? What about the people that came to him to learn about their own great grandparents and great-great- grandparents when no one else could tell them about them? My grandpa was a vault of knowledge; it was just that he did not go to a regular school. The question remained; how was it that he wanted me to be put into a trade school instead of a regular one? How did my own father get his own education? This was what I would need to look into a whole lot more, more questions for my Dad. I concluded from this story meteoric that my grandfather was illiterate.

Chapter 2

I became friends with Ciji in elementary school. We all found out that he liked to say "My name is Ciji." He would walk up to you during recess or break and utter those four words so softly that they sounded appealing—like part of a song, only very short. So everybody knew the boy named Ciji. He was one of the saddest looking people I'd ever met. He was also very friendly and kind. I still marvel at the blatant irony in this person. How in the world do you keep up a sad look while bestowing kindness and friendship? I was dumbfounded by this.

Ciji was kind of small for his age. He said he was ten years old, but he looked more like eight. He also looked cute with his curly brown hair and dark blue eyes that looked a little black when he was excited. His eyes shone when he was amused. His skin looked pale, as if he needed some sun. It was generally believed that Ciji could have been, as he spent a good amount of time in the sun. Sometimes, he had a bleak look that rapidly change to bewilderment in his eyes.

Ciji never talked about himself. He rarely answered questions about his parents or siblings. He never revealed where he lived or how many siblings he had. He was very nice, though, and he played with everybody. We all enjoyed his company, because he was fun to be around. But each day on the way to school, he would join us from the exact same place and then would leave us from the same place on the way home from school. This place happened to be a little more than halfway to our school.

On the way to school, it seemed like he appeared from nowhere around that particular area. On the way home, it looked like he always did a disappearing act as soon as we reached that same spot. At first, we all thought this happened because we were not paying attention. There was always a bunch of kids in our group, but the crowd decreased in size as we walked further away from school.

People left the group as we approached their houses. Most would wave and say goodbye as they left and then run toward the path that led to their houses. Some just waved and would run right home if their houses were by the roadside. Ciji never said a word; he would just quietly disappear from the group. At first, I thought I was the only one who noticed this. That was until my other friend said something. It was on a Friday, Caro called Ciji's name but turned to find he'd already gone. We were all speechless. Ciji had been walking with us a few moments before, until we passed a cocoa tree. This tree had so many leaves and fruits that we went back to see if Ciji was just hiding behind it. He wasn't. Why did we find Ciji fun to be with? I really couldn't pinpoint the reasons. Maybe it was because he was somewhat strange and mysterious. I ponder about this from time to time and I was still flabbergasted by it all.

Chapter 3

Ciji has been my friend since fifth grade. He said his family had just moved here from the South. We had been going to school together for almost a year before I realized that he sort of disappeared at will—mostly on the way back from school. My other friends lived down the street. We had been to one another's houses. Ciji was the only one who always had an excuse; he always came up with a reason why we couldn't go to his house. One time, he said his parents were away. Another time, he said there was construction work being done in his house. There was always a reason that we couldn't hang out with him at his house. This made us even more curious to go to his house to play. Also we were very eager to explore Ciji's tricks on the way home from school. He was subtle about it. We implored him to let us come to his house. Our effort to persuade him was fruitless.

So on the way home from school—together as usual—the four of us made our way toward home. Caro, Chima, and I had already made up our minds that day to catch Ciji in his disappearing act. So, as we neared the shrubs at the beginning of my street, Ciji quickly ran behind the cocoa tree. We were all ready for him, so we ran after him. Just when we realized what was happening, it was too late again; he was nowhere to be found. We believed in magic, so we checked the leaves and fruits to make sure he hadn't turned into a fly or something. There was nothing. We all went home thinking that there had to be a better way to find out what was going on. We decided to ask Ciji about it. It was customary for us to spend recess time together. We refused to allow Ciji's disappearing acts erode our friendship with him.

When I played soccer with my dad that evening, I suddenly found myself telling him about the mystery of Ciji. I said, "Dad there's this friend in school who disappears behind a cocoa tree every day on the way home from school. He always joins us on the way to school from the same area every morning."

"And you have not been able to see where he comes from or from what direction he joins you?" my dad asked. I shook my head as if to avert attention before answering.

"No," I said, "Because he always comes running behind us."

"Have you tried waiting for him around there while paying great attention to your surroundings?" he asked. My father stood upright and touched my arm.

"Yes. We end up getting to school late, only to find he's already in class," I said in frustration.

"Your friend sounds like the kid I had growing up myself. Has your Dede told you his own story that sounds like yours?" I shook my head. We called my grandfather, Dede.

"Maybe it is the right time to ask him about it. It seems like we all had the same kind of friend as children." I stood there, my heart throbbing at the mere thought of this. There was a legitimate concern and hunger to acquire more knowledge about this matter.

What are the odds of this being true? I mean about having the *same exact experience* as my dad and his dad. That night, I went to bed with a feeling of slight tingling. I was thrilled that I might have had a story similar to that of my grandfather.

Chapter 4

I looked up to Dede so much that I thought he knew everything. In the corner of my heart, apprehension lurked in trickles. I realized I was only dreaming about hanging out with him because I heard a knock on my door. My mom yelled, "Obi, it's seven o'clock already!" I opened my eyes; I would be hurrying to school soon. Maybe Ciji would let us hang out at his house today. I quickly washed up and prepared for school. As I ran out of the house, I was joined by Caro and Chima. They, too, were eager to see Ciji again. As soon as we reached the shrub area near the beginning of our street, we all slowed down. We had accelerated our speed so much that we reached the nearby prairie sooner than usual. Then I watched as Caro fell headlong into the grass because of her speed before jumping up and bursting into a mirth. We just smiled at her.

"Should we gather around the cocoa tree and wait?" Caro asked.

"No need," I said. "We will end up getting to school late; you know what happened each time we did that." We learnt the hard way, after each gruelling wait near the cocoa tree, we would up late for school only to find Ciji is already in class.

"Let's continue going to school. If he appears behind us, we shall see," Chima said. We went slowly past the cocoa tree, and sure enough, Ciji came up behind us. He appeared mellow and completely unaware of the obnoxious problem he was causing among us.

So I turned to him and said, "Hi, Ciji. Don't tell me you are a cocoa boy. You never let us come to your house; you disappear behind this tree every day on the way home from school." To my surprise, Ciji looked down and kept walking beside us. He didn't say anything and neither did we. During recess, I gave him one of his favorite treats; a cupcake with sprinkles. My mother sometimes made them. It was the least I could do before I pelt him with all the pending questions lurking under my tongue like a docile body of water whose momentum was held down by a levee.

Ciji thanked me and brought me aside. "Would it be enough if I told you that a family secret was why I couldn't bring you to my house?" he asked quietly. He implored with his eyes. The flood of words behind my tongue was beginning to recede but I caught myself in time.

"No." I answered. "You will have to come up with a better explanation." I tried very hard to mate that resort as trivial as possible.

"Okay, are you able to keep a secret?" he asked. His voice was urgent as I mulled on this.

"Yes," I said. I realized that my friends left the responsibility of convincing Ciji to me and I was not about to shirk that vacation.

"Then I will show you where I live, but if you tell other people, my family may have to move away again. Don't bother to call law enforcement; we are law abiding citizens," he said. I started watching the clock, looking forward to school dismissal. It took forever, but eventually the bell rang; it was the end of the school day. I grabbed my bag and ran outside. The sun seemed to shine brighter that day. I forgot that we always walked from school with two other friends. I was so excited to learn about Ciji's secret that I had forgotten about Caro and Chima. It wasn't for long, though; they both joined us on the way home, and my heart promptly sank at the sight of them. I wondered if Ciji would still show me his house in front of the others. I went into a random rant as I tried to convince my friends to be discreet with any secret Ciji would show or tell us.

As we neared the cocoa tree and the other shrubs, I turned to Ciji and said, "You know I've known Caro and Chima since third grade, and I can tell you that they can both keep secrets. Whatever you tell us today will not be revealed to anybody else unless you give us permission to do so." I realized the magnitude of my request to him as soon as I made it. I waited to hear the status of my request.

To my surprise he said "No problem." Then he made the three of us raise our right pinkies up and promise not to tell another soul what he was about to show us. We all promised.

Ciji then looked around quickly and brought us to the cocoa tree. Of course, we all knew this cocoa tree, but what he did next took all of us by surprise.

Chapter 5

Ciji quickly bent down and with a sweep of his left hand, he pressed some plants away from the base of the cocoa tree and said, "Watch this." We all peered into the base of the tree but saw nothing. "You don't see anything here?" he said. We all replied no in unison. Then he thought for a moment and said, "Ooh, sorry my mistake."

Then he brought out a notebook from his school bag, scribbled something on one page, then asked us to read it aloud. It read something like *cocoa door*. Caro, Chima, and I read the two words aloud and immediately saw a small spot where Ciji was pointing to the base of the cocoa tree; it looked like a small red window. Ciji said it was the door. Then he asked us if we still wanted to go to his house. We apprehensively agreed. By now, I had already pinched myself twice to make sure I wasn't dreaming. I thought of my maternal uncle as I did this, he was the one that taught me to this wherever I couldn't differentiate between dream and reality.

I looked at Caro. She looked a little frightened, so I asked her if she really wanted to go to Ciji's house. She said yes, but her voice was a little shaky.

Then I turned to Chima. In a very small voice he said, "Yes. I want to go to Ciji's house, but is he even human? I would hate to be eaten by some kind of monster; my parents would die with grief." This was a little disappointing to me on one hand and hilarious on the other. We have been begging Ciji to bring us to his house to play and now we were scared to go there.

So I turned to Ciji. He said, "We don't eat humans, but if you like I can tell you my story today and then bring you to my house to play—only when you are ready. It has to be on a day my parents would not be around, though." Ciji proceeded to tell us about his family.

It turned out that Ciji was the ghost of a boy named Ciji who had died at the age of ten doing terrible things. From then on, he had been ten years old for over four hundred years. Ciji revealed to us that he might have been friends with our great-grandparents, grandparents, and parents when they were our age. Ciji explained that his parents had been bad people before they died. This was why they all had to wait in their current state until they had done enough good deeds to earn themselves a state of rest. I thought this was a tragedy in itself.

His parents spent every day helping people who were currently alive. This was the only way they could make up for the evils they had done while still alive on earth. This was why his parents where always very busy. Ciji himself also helped people whenever he could so that he could start having a perfect rest. He and his parents were what we knew as *ghosts* on Earth.

By this time, I had more questions than answers. As Ciji continued to talk, many things didn't add up. Then suddenly, he said that he had to go home, and he asked if any of us had any questions. Well, we all had questions for Ciji. As I looked at him, I tried to imagine what it was like to live like a ghost—whether he was able to really eat, drink, sleep, cry, laugh, or feel anything like humans do. I told Ciji we would ask questions the next day; it was also past the time we had to be home.

Chapter 6

As we scurried home to our families, I kept thinking about Ciji's story. *If Ciji has been ten years old for four hundred years, then he must be four hundred and ten years old,* I thought. *If that was the case he must be very wise. Did this mean he had lived in every continent known to man? How did they travel? How could anybody fit into that tiny door in the tree that looked more like a small dot? What had they done to earn this life of limbo? How many more years were left for them to serve before they could be in peace? Would they ever be able to rest in peace? Would they ever be able to rest?* And the questions went on and on in my head. What about the paradise that people sometimes talked about? What disqualified Ciji and his family from entering it?

Before crawling into bed, I wondered if Ciji was an only child and if any of his family was able to rest in peace at all. I was so tired that I slept peacefully until morning with no bad dreams—in fact no dreams at all. I scrambled out of bed and prepared for school so quickly that my mother noticed. "I think our son is growing up quickly," she said to my dad. "I did not have to wake him up today. He breezed through his morning routine."

"Maybe he has something on his mind," my father replied. My parents knew me better than I knew myself. It was as if their love and knowledge of me intensified as I grew older. In spite of my age, they pampered me more and more.

I ran out the door with my school bag hanging from my right shoulder and quickly waved goodbye to my parents before disappearing into the morning light. The weather looked gloomy. There were dark clouds here and there that made it look like it was going to rain, so I ran as quickly as I could. I heard Chima calling Caro's name, and I turned to see her trying to catch up with him. They both looked like they had something on their minds, as I'm sure I did. We all walked on in silence; nobody wanted to start a conversation. Then I wondered if they had the same questions I had. As we walked past the cocoa tree, Ciji hastily joined us, and—as if he could read our minds—he said, "Don't worry, I will answer all your questions after school." We had all wanted to throw our questions at him as soon as we saw him. My courageous front was just a sham but that didn't prevent me from wanting to ask questions.

After all, we had been patient enough to hold our questions until then. I didn't know about Caro and Chima, but I was bursting with questions. It even crossed my mind to find out from Ciji if anything bad would happen to us if we told anyone about his story. I had never kept any secret from my father until then. Even though I promised not to tell anyone Ciji's story, I had to find a way of telling my parents without saying any names or being specific. Maybe I could say that I had heard a story going around in school about there being some ghosts in the next town. I looked at Ciji as these questions went through my mind. I could never guess what was going on in *his* mind, mainly because he always looked sad. He always had dark circles around his eyes.

This made me begin to wonder if Ciji ever slept. Did ghosts ever sleep at night? Or did they have to haunt houses all night long? What about the stories we had heard about ghosts making some weird noise? Did Ciji do this, too? As I sat down in class, I knew it would take a lot of effort to concentrate on school work that day.

Chapter 7

I sat in class all morning trying not to think about Ciji's story. For a moment, I would pay full attention to what the teacher was saying, and then—without any warning—I would start thinking about the cocoa door or ghosts. More and more questions came up in my mind for Ciji. It seemed like my mind was trying to remind me of the questions to ask Ciji after school. Then I realized that Mrs. Thatcher was talking to me. I was able to hear the end of the question and my name, so I looked at her and said, "Excuse me?"

"I see you have something on your mind, Obi. Could you share this with the rest of the class?" she prompted.

I stood up, dumbfounded. I was not going to tell her Ciji's story, and I certainly wasn't telling it to the whole class. So I quickly thought of an answer, one that would not make me look stupid. I glanced at the chalkboard and realized we were on Social Studies. I said I was wondering what a basic family looked like four hundred years ago. She replied, "It is a good thing to have a curious mind, but don't forget that paying attention in class helps you do better on exams. How can you understand something if you did not pay attention when it was being explained?" Then she continued to teach, and I took a breath of relief. Now, something had to be done about Ciji's secret. I had already started lying to my teacher all because of it. I could not go on like this. It was as if I was negligent in class, this flaw made my insides feel as if they were not mine. I was starting to be numb on the inside, this was bad, very, very bad.

The morning went by in a blur. I hoped I would be able to ask Ciji some of the questions I had during break. The bell for recess was a welcome relief to me. I could not wait to start. As soon as Ciji joined me, the barrage of questions began. It was like a gate was opened for a flood. Ciji was very patient with me. He asked me to wait for Chima and Caro, as they might have the same questions that I had. It turned out he was right; they both had similar questions to mine. The three of us were worried and eager to know if there would be any consequences if we broke our promise to keep silent. Ciji sat down with us in the school playground to answer our questions. His eyes changed from time to time as he talked to us. Sometimes they looked excited and shiny. It turned out that ghosts were very different from humans. To become a ghost, a human being would have to die first. To be in a horrible position like Ciji's, the human being must have been a bad person when they were alive. If they killed other people while they were alive, they came back as ghosts of animals. If they destroyed other people's property when they were human beings, they also became ghosts of animals when they died. If they knew that their friends or family members were killing people or destroying property and did nothing about it, they became ghosts that would take care of the animal ghosts for years and years. Ciji was about to talk some more when the bell rang again. Recess was over. We all took deep breaths and went back to our classes. We had been holding our breaths without knowing it.

Chapter 8

After school that day, we all walked toward home in anticipation. Ciji promised to bring us to his house to play. His parents were not home. Friday was the day they worked harder than other days. Ciji also promised to finish his story as we walked. He thought it would be clearer to us if we saw what he was talking about. As we reached the shrub area, we walked straight to the cocoa tree at the center. Ciji again used his left hand to brush aside some plants at the base of the tree. Chima, Caro, and I all said "cocoa door" at the count of three. Then the tiny red dot appeared again. Ciji touched our right hands as in a handshake, and we all walked through the cocoa door. This was the first time I was able to walk through a closed door; it felt like we had flown through the tree. We hurtled through the vista but were unscathed as we reached the other side. There seemed to be a magnetic force drawing us to the other side. Soon, we saw ourselves standing in a town that looked dull and awful. Where is the geographical location of this place? I wondered.

First there were pigs crying *oink, oink, oink*—all the while covered in sewage. They stank. Before I could open my mouth to ask a question that had come to my mind, Ciji said he had to put some plant pulp on us. He quickly plucked three leaves from a nearby shrub—the only live plant in this village—and pressed them between his palms, turning them into a gray pulp. Then he rubbed a small amount on each our foreheads.

"This will hide your human smell," he said. "I don't want them to know I brought human beings here. Yeah, and about the pigs, these are the ghosts of people who killed many people at once. As you can see, some were adults and some were children. They don't eat anything until night time. This was the time the phretas (someone that did nothing to prevent the attack on innocent people even though they knew about it before it happened) took them to eat sewage from the earth. The pigs continued in pig form for up to two hundred years, and then they become ghosts like me and the others." Phretas was a hybrid between ghosts and aliens in the way they look. Phretas did not commit any homicide but failed to report the plan of others even though they knew about it. Phretas supervised all the others. They also admonish the human looking ghosts to do good. Phretas also beseech the ghosts to good

"What about the dogs? Are they also ghosts?" I could not resist asking.

"Yes," said Ciji. "These are the ghosts of people who killed children, pregnant women, or disabled people. As in the case of the pigs, these dogs continue this way for two hundred years, become ghosts, and then try to help people so they can start resting in peace. This could take as long as eight hundred years. All the chickens, fowls, birds you see here are the ghosts of people who destroyed other people's property before they died. They too continue like this for two hundred years, then turn into ghosts and start serving and helping people until they do enough to start resting. The goats are the ghosts of all liars and people that committed perjury. They would continue as these for two hundred years, then become ghosts. You see how lean these animals all seem. This is because nobody was authorized to feed them until night. So, that is why they all look starved. If any of the ghosts tried to feed them, they would be punished. They would instantly turn into the kind of animal ghost they were trying to feed. I came here as a ghost because I was supposed to kill people, but I ended up injuring some. They all eventually recovered in the hospital, but I died a few months after the attack, so I came here as a ghost. "One of my uncles was already here before we arrived. It turned out he came here as a phretas. At first, there were feelings of disappointment on every side. Ghosts were appalled at the state of things here. Where were the promises made to us while we were still alive? Where were the twelve girls, the mansions, and other grand things they told us would be ours if we complied with their commands? The empty promises were immediately replaced with feelings of melancholy. Any questions we had were answered by the phretas; it turned out that doing bad things earns you nothing good. Rather, you get thrown into this life of limbo where you feel the sadness and agony of those innocent people you killed. The pain you feel seems unending indeed. What a miserable way to spend your afterlife." This sounded grimy to me.

"What did the dogs eat?" asked Chima. The dogs were very grimy.

"They fed on the pigs' poop in the night. All day long, they had nothing to eat or drink. They drank the pigs' pee at night, too," replied Ciji. Ciji then explained that *Phretas* could be used as singular for one of them, or plural for more than one. It stood for the ghosts of adults who didn't report a wrong done by another person, or who were aware of a plot that someone did against someone else, but did nothing to prevent this wrong. Ciji then explained that killings done during a time of war did not count. Nobody got punished after death for defending the masses.

Ciji's

Chapter 9

Ciji gave us a brief preview of what to expect to see here. We all stood in awe as we listened to Ciji. It crossed my mind that I wouldn't want to be a ghost if this was how they lived. We had been walking down Ciji's street all this time. We went past many houses that looked abandoned. There were no live trees that we could see. There were a lot of dried dead shrubs; little trees without leaves or life. They looked as if they would fall if one touched them. There was neither grass nor plants of any kind. Everywhere looked dry. The streets were dirt roads. Once or twice we passed by strange creatures that looked like monsters. It was nothing like what I had ever seen on earth—I mean, in the world of the living.

We made a right turn and came face to face with one of the worst houses I'd ever seen. The color was washed as if the house had not been painted in years. In front of it was the number 1265 written numerically. Ciji said, "This is my house." He merely pushed the door open; there was no door knob. The door swung open with a terrible noise.

We all went inside. My heart began to race even more than it had since entering Ciji's world. I was both eager and afraid at the same time. Was Ciji taking us into a house full of ghosts, monsters, or witches that eat small children? Well, Ciji's world was full of surprises.

First, I noticed that there were no stairs from the street into the house. Not even one. You just stepped into the house on the same level as the street. Second, there were no rooms like in the houses where we lived; there was just one big space. Third, there were no chairs. "Everybody sits on the ground," Ciji told us. As we all sat on the floor, I noticed there were only two items in the whole house: a standing clock that took up one quarter of the space in the house and a small glass that looked like a mirror.

This clock was nothing like the ones I had seen before. It had seven hands. The longest one counted years, the second one counted months, the third hand counted weeks, the fourth counted days, the fifth counted hours, the sixth counted minutes, and the seventh counted seconds. I was more familiar with the last three. I was hoping that Ciji would explain the use of this timepiece to us.

Meanwhile, I noticed that the floor was warm as we sat down. Sometimes, we heard echoes of people crying and moaning. At other times, we thought we could hear the crackling of flames from a fire. Before I could open my mouth to ask more questions, Caro beat me to it.

"How did you come by such a huge clock?" she asked.

"All the houses have them. Every one year, the year bell rings; counting up to the number of years served," Ciji replied. "This way you know how long you have served," he added.

"Is that a mirror?" I quickly asked.

"No," Ciji answered. "It is more like a glass we use to see into the ground." Suddenly I remembered the warm floor.

"What is there in the ground to see?" I asked.

"The ground is where all the people that died while doing a bad deed ended up. They will never be able to leave, and that place is their home forever," Ciji answered. "Do you want to see?"

We all eagerly replied yes. So Ciji took the "glass" from the foot of the clock and placed it carefully on the floor. We were quite fascinated by what we saw, and I would never forget the horror.

Everywhere was filled with fire, and it looked like people were inside the fire. Their bodies were full of bugs that were eating their flesh. The fire was also burning their flesh. So, I asked the next question that came to my mind. "Why don't they die from this fire?"

"Because they were already dead before going there. What you see are their souls. They will live forever in this hole," Ciji answered.

I saw anguish and pain on their faces. It seemed like I could even smell the smoke and decay. I had thought my grandfather knew everything, but now I realized that Ciji knew a whole lot more. Then again, my grandfather was just seventy-five years old while Ciji was 410. "I will help you home now; you have seen my house," Ciji said.

As he led us back to the outside of the cocoa tree, Chima said, "Awesome, but sad. I wouldn't want to live there." He had just echoed what was on my mind, too. As we headed home, I became more determined than ever to be a good boy.

That night, I went to bed with many questions on my mind—all for Ciji, I mean. Then I remembered that he promised to tell us more about himself if we could keep everything he said secret.

1265

Chapter 10

AN ANCIENT GHOST

So now we have formed the habit of going to Ciji's village almost every friday after school. Although we spend at least one hour each time we went over there, we still feel strange being there. Ciji has been kind enough to answer all our questions. We all agreed that some of the questions we had for him were very intrusive while the other ones sounded foolish. So sometimes, we may start a question this way; "Ciji, I'm sorry this question sounds stupid but…". Whenever we start a question that way, Ciji always shrugged before saying to us that no question is a stupid question.

"Ghosts like me don't have to eat". He answered.

Unlike human beings that need to eat to maintain their bodies, we eat only if we want to, we don't need to eat. We eat when we need to ward off suspicion or prevent the spread of rumours about us. We try to eat when people offer us something to eat but the food we eat go straight to void. There is no digestion; no possibility of overeating; no need to use the bathroom to pee or to poo. We can eat as much as we want without fear of weight gain or anything like that. Any ghost that is in the shape of a human being does not need to eat."

"But the ones that have the shape of animals really need to eat. It's been noticed that these ghosts that took the shape of animals become very lean and ghastly without proper nourishment. Their ribs start showing on each side beneath their hide, their necks stretched out in long thin frames. Each one showing real signs of emaciation and hunger. Their four legs touching the ground like four pieces of dry sticks blended perfectly with the ground and the surroundings."

"Those kinds of ghosts also pass waste materials like real animals. They feel heat and cold like them, too." I watched Ciji's face as he explained all these; we nodded as everything became clearer to us. His eyes twinkled a little bit as he went on, then turned from deep black to bluish grey from time to time, as evidence of the deep emotion he was having as he spoke about his people. Finally, his eyes blended with the environment as he stopped speaking.

Then I asked the next question that came into my mind.

"Do you remember all your friends from the time you became a ghost?" Ciji looked at me briefly and then looked straight past me as if he was either thinking about something or trying to remember his past friends from the time he became a ghost. We all waited and watched as he quietly looked at his spread out fingers before raising his eyes again to look at our inquisitive faces. Then, Caro cleared her throat and said "Please tell us if you remember any of them." Ciji then sighed and said, "It is very difficult not to remember my past friends since 1604 A.D."

Sometimes, I remember them so clearly that I wonder if my mind became sharper after I became a ghost."

"So, please tell us about them", begged Chima.

"Well, for starters, I would like you to know that I have lived in almost all the continents known to man, almost all." Ciji replied

"My family have had to move whenever people found out who we really are. Each time our cover is blown, we hastily leave the area. We always moved before the pointing became too much. One time, the kids were walking up to me and pinching me to see if I reacted to this. At another time, people were walking up to me and asking me point blank

"Is it true you are a ghost?"

Ciji took a deep breath and quietly mused.

"We moved away as soon as people found out we were ghosts." "This time I am hoping that we would not have to move away from here any time soon. You see, I like it here and we have lived here for almost one hundred and seventy-five years; this is the most we have ever lived in one place. The people here are pleasant and less noisy than the rest of the world."

Ciji stared straight into space, pausing for a minute or two.

"So, Obi I grew up with your grandfather and your father, too. I was there as they were each growing up; playing with each one as they were growing up in the clearing near the village square. I watched your grandfather grow taller and taller, the same with your dad. I never grow any taller or fatter than the day we moved here. We have a secret to keep people from recognizing us or remembering that I was the same boy who played with the older generation." Now Ciji's eyes turned black as charcoals while they lit up as smoldering cedars all at the same time; his eyes ended up looking like the center of a campfire in the night. Ciji's eyes were always fascinating to watch as he told his peculiar story.

He turned his face towards me as if he was gauging the effect of his stories on me. His demeanor became very grave for a fleeting moment then, he smiled and said, "But the ones that I watched growing up before my eyes were always good people."

"My family was able to stay on in this place because the few people that found out about my family accepted us the way we were and refused to carry about the tale".

"It feels awesome to know people that are like that. They kept the secret." Now, I became perplexed by this part of his story, and I began to wonder what he meant exactly by this. Does this mean that my father knew that Ciji was a ghost all along but kept quiet? What about my grandfather? How could both of them be so secretive about this? I know quite well that my grandfather was not educated. So I asked Ciji my next question.

"Ciji, tell me again who among my family were you friends with before me?"

"I sort of played with your grandfather as he was growing up but I went to middle school with your dad." Ciji gave me this answer without much thought.

"Were you friends with our fathers too?", asked both Caro and Chima at the same time. To which Ciji replied, "Yes" and "No".

Then he went ahead to explain, "Chima, your father wasn't around here at the time so I didn't know him when he was a child. Caro, yes, I was friends with your dad in primary school. We usually played together with the other children. In all these years, none of my friends ever followed me home until now."

Then Chima mused.

"I guess dad was still in Japan at that time".

After this, we all decided it was time to go home to human land and Ciji came with us and helped us through the cocoa tree before going back to his own village. On the side of our village, it was getting dark; somehow we have forgotten about time as we listened earnestly to Ciji.

Chapter 11

THE BASILYNTH SHRUB

Today is Friday and we prepared eagerly for school with thoughts of playing with Ciji in his village at the back of our minds. I thought of Ciji's scary village and the risk of his parents coming home and finding us there and came to the conclusion that these trips to Ciji's house were scary and made my stomach queasy to say the least. Still, even though we were somewhat afraid to see the things in Ciji's village, we were excited to go there, yes, we were excited to visit with Ciji in his village.

By now, we are familiar with the leafy cocoa tree with some ripe and unripe pods spread out all over the tree in rows. This tree became a friendly and welcoming site to us because we passed through it twice every Friday on our way to and from Ciji's house. This tree remained a fascinating object to us; it was no longer as scary as it used to be in my own opinion. After school, as we were walking behind Ciji towards this tree, there appeared to be something that looked like some bird's nests in this tree and the cawing like that of some birds. This caused us to hurry towards the tree, we leaped towards this cocoa tree without even realizing it. We panted as we reached this tree. We were out of breath and disinclined to chat as we looked on in wonder at what we found living in the nests. For a moment, we gazed on these nests wondering. One of the nests was shaped like a boot with brown colored straws all interwoven and criss-crossed in the most beautiful way. A beautiful white and blue feathered bird was standing on the mouth of this nest. The other nest was in the crotch of the cocoa tree, this nest was more roundish and open on top like a small bowl made from green strands of straws and leaves. Inside this nest were bluish eggs, five in number. The black bird, crow, that was doing most of the cawing was also walking around the eggs in a circular motion. The nests on this tree, the birds on it and the tree did not make it any scarier than before. We are now familiar shrubs. We even grew familiar with the lone green shrub that has leaves that help hide our smell from the nest of the ghosts in Ciji's village.

I noticed something strange about this shrub. It did not grow taller than it was. No new leaves grew on this shrub. The number of leaves left after we used some remained the same. So I worried about what we will use if the leaves run out on this shrub. Ciji had been plucking leaves of this shrub, rubbing it into a pulp between his palms and putting it on each of our foreheads before taking us into his village. Ciji called this shrub "basilcynth" adding this, "The leaves smell like basil and hyacinth combined". We all agreed with this. This shrub really smelled like he said.

As we got ready to enter Ciji's village, Ciji plucked one leaf of basilcynth and made it into a pulp as he rubbed his palms together briefly for a minute. Then he applied the pulp briefly to my forehead, Caro's forehead and Chima's also. I counted the remaining leaves on this shrub and there were only five leaves left. The first thought that went through my mind was the word five. I mean the number 5.

The second thought I had was that five leaves equals five visits; meaning that we will use up all the leaves in five more visits to Ciji's village and then what? I thought about the excitement we feel in visiting Ciji's house and how empty our Fridays will become if we stopped visiting Ciji; I trembled a little as I thought about this. We will not be able to visit without applying this leaf; this leaf is what hide our human smell from the ghosts in Ciji's place. The third thing that went through my mind was the thought of going to school every day and finding that Ciji no longer goes there. I know that as soon as the ghosts realise that people have discovered their land, they would all have to move yet to another part of the world. I would hate to be one of the people that caused such a problem for Ciji. Lastly, I wondered what the other ghosts will do to Ciji and his family when they find out that Ciji was the one that brought humans to their land. So I asked Ciji this question as soon as we reached his house.

"Ciji, what happens in a few weeks when all the basilcynth leaves get used up?"

He thought for a second and said, "May be we can look for similar shrub in other places". I wasn't quite satisfied with the answer so I decided to take matters into my own hands. I thought that I could bring some of the roots or leaves home to my own village and have the village gardener work on replicating this plant.

So on our way home from Ciji's house, I stole a leaf and a small stringed root off of the basilcynth, the only plant known to us that was capable of hiding us from the ghost in shadowland. I made sure no one saw me take it and I quickly slipped them into my shorts pocket. At first, it felt weird taking something that is not mine but on second thought, I saw this as a move to help myself and my friends maintain a tradition that we recently acquired. A tradition that has brought much needed excitement into our lives. More importantly, this new tradition made the bond between us friends stronger. I will just hand this root and leaf over to the gardener, who happens to be my neighbor, and ask him to help grow more of those.

As soon as I reached home, I hid the strand and leaf beside the flower pot on my porch before going into my house. Too tired from the trip to Ciji's place, I spoke only a few words during dinner and I was very glad to dive under the covers in my bed moments later. I fell asleep almost immediately. As soon as I woke up and heard the crow of the cock, I quickly ran outside to bring my root strand and leaf to the gardener.

I retrieved them from beside the flower pot and reached my neighbor's house as speedily as possible. As I turned into my neighbor's compound I saw him working on his front yard garden as usual. I yelled out, "Hi", stepped up to him with the basilcynth leaf and root in my hand. He said hi to me. But as soon as he saw what I had in my hand, he whooped and started walking backwards, taking backward steps as if he wanted to put a huge distance between him and the leaf and root. Then from a distance he yelled

"Please stay away from me, don't come near me with that thing in your hand." Then he ran back into his house and shut the door so hard that I became confused. Now, my neighbor has got me wondering why he was behaving so strangely because of a little leaf and root. So I put the root and leaf back into my pocket and went and knocked on Mr. Morgan Gadner's front door, calling out his name at the same time.

"Mr. Gadner, Mr. Gadner, I didn't mean to scare you, honestly". I stopped knocking and listened for a moment. "It is only a leaf and small root of a basilcynth leaf, I just wanted to see if you can grow it in your garden, that is all".

I started hearing some muffled noise from within the house and it sounded like someone was sobbing uncontrollably. Thinking that this must be Mr. Morgan Gadner. I continued to talk to him in a calming way. "Mr. Gadner, I also wanted to find out if you can help tell me where I can find this plant or how I can grow one successfully. I didn't mean to cause any trouble". The sobbing stopped as suddenly as it started and the subsequent silence was heavy and ominous. I waited a few more minutes and decided to leave him alone. That became the last time anyone saw or heard from Mr. Gadner. After a few days, my parents called law enforcement and requested that they do a well check on our neighbor. The police knocked on his door, silence. They finally pushed the door open found the house empty; no Mr. Morgan Gardner, no chairs, no sofas, no carpet, no furniture at all. There was no sign that anybody had lived there up until few days ago. The woman that was Mr. Gadner's wife was nowhere to be found. The little boy that was their child was nowhere to be found. The police letter tried to locate any Morgan Gadner that ever lived and discovered that there was one Morgan Gadner born in 1809 AD who died in 1872 AD. The library even had a record of a headstone and burial site for this guy. This Morgan Gadner never had any child or family before his death. Mr. Gadner, our neighbor, the village gardener who was known for his kindness and good works throughout the village, vanished till this day.

Now I realised there must be something extraordinary about the plant leaf and root. I decided to take this leaf and root whenever I go, who knows where I might stumble upon people that could help me find where else this plant grows. I brought the leaf and root to the teacher that taught natural studies also known as Science and she stopped coming to school the day after she saw the leaf and root. Her neighbors said she left in a pretty big hurry and has never been seen or heard from since.

Suddenly, it crossed my mind that the leaf and root might be taking people away from us. Finally, I brought this leaf and root to my church. I briefly thought about confiding in my parents about basilcynth or showing it to them but then I remembered that Ciji does not even know that I have part of this plant with me and that something drastic is happening whenever I showed it to people. As we sang hymns inside the church, I kept hoping that my parents will not leave in a hurry if they see this leaf.

One hour into the church service, the pastor called for testimony. I immediately jumped up from my seat and ran to the altar. Putting my hand into the pocket of my dress shirt, I quickly brought out the leaf and root. I started waving them in the air with my right hand for all eyes to see. I paused to watch the reaction of people to this. While my parents looked at each other and my siblings mouthed, "What is he doing?"

Some other families looked surprised but all waited to hear my testimony. Everywhere became quiet as people got ready to hear what God did for me. I continued to wave the leaf and the root in the sight of everyone. Meanwhile, there were gasps that came from both the pulpit and pew.

People were getting up and leaving the church in a hurry never to be heard from or seen again. At least one quarter of the congregation left. Even the assistant pastor also left with his family and was never seen or heard from again. I kept my eyes on my parents and siblings but none of them left. I kept my eyes on my parents and siblings but none of them left. So much for the message the assistant pastor has been preaching about paradise. As the senior pastor started to quieten people down, I put back the leaf and root into my pocket as I ran out from church, myself. This is to avoid questions that may lead to exposing Ciji and shadowland. I didn't have anything or story prepared for this and I also didn't want anyone else to get hold of this leaf and root. On reaching home, I planted both the leaf and the root strand in one of our flower pots but my mind kept going through the thought of what might happen if the rest of the village saw this basilcynth. I made a strong determination not to reveal shadowland to anybody, not to my parents ,my sibling and certainly not to my pastor. This means that I must act very dumb or forgetful when somebody asks about the incident at the church.

Chapter 12

LITTERS, LITTERS, WHAT A SHAME, CARO'S STORY

Ciji has been helping a lot in our town and neighboring towns also, but one of the ways he helped the town really stood out and made him unforgettable. My home town was known for the trashed look of some parts of town especially the prairie near my house. Ciji helped minimize littering around here, but no, he did not pick up after people. He did not put up signs urging people to clean up after themselves; there were already signboards advising people that they will be fined for littering. Obviously, these signs did not deter people from littering. People were throwing litter on the street floors, from their houses, from their school bags, while others simply throw trash on the ground instead of into trash bins situated in visible places around town. It seems that nobody is paying attention to the signboards or the trash bins.

Ciji sometimes come to play with us in my house but as time went on, the littering problem only got worse. There reached a time that the streets near my house were so full of trash that it became difficult to see where to put our feet to walk to our house. We were finding it difficult to determine if the ground was level or not before taking each step. We were stepping into all sorts of things like leftover food that stank really bad, used towels, tissues, torn clothes, torn bags, damaged toys.

This was when Ciji decided that something has to be done. He remained thoughtful as we reached my house. He also looked absent- minded as we hung out with him so that I ended up asking him what was on his mind to which he replied, "I guess we need to take matters into our own hands about this town's littering problem." Ciji soon snapped out his quietude and started acting as the Ciji we know. He joined in on our conversations as he was to do. I let out a sigh of relief and noticed that my other friends were also relieved.

Ciji asked us to help him stop these pigs from littering the town. We let Ciji know that we were perturbed and were willing to help in any way possible. Ciji advised us to wear parkas to school tomorrow and be ready to work with one mind. He revealed that what we need to do required unity to be effective. The step we would take towards the cleanliness of our surroundings must be taken between 12noon and 3pm, must be done at the center of town and must be done for three consecutive days. This meant we must all figure out the center of town and proceed these everyday after school for three days in a row for whatever we did to be effective.

Our school dismissal time was 1:50pm Monday to Friday. So Tuesday after school, we all headed for the center of town. Ciji found out the real center of town and we all headed there immediately after school. Ciji had written something down on a piece of paper and asked each one of us to say the words written there in unison while holding hands. We only need to say the words three times in unison. We started this procedure Tuesday around 2:30pm. It took us less than 15 minutes to finish the process. We completed everything by Thursday 2:40pm

On this Thursday, as soon as we finished the procedure, on our way back from the center of town, we started noticing that the streets were actually neat and clean. There were no more piles of trash laying in the streets. We were beaming with joy as we went on but soon realized that there were uproars in the streets, brawls? There was pandemonium here and there; people gathered together; others yelling on top of their lungs and others antagonizing and exchanging blows.

We decided to go near one of the more peaceful crowd to see what was going on. As we were getting nearer and nearer to this crowd we heard one of the men saying this, "I don't know what is going on but I left an empty cup of coffee on the ground in the street but found it on my bed when I entered my house."

Another one said that all the trash he had thrown into the street were piled up on his favorite chair this afternoon as he entered his house. A casual bystander looked on. "At first I didn't know what it was all about", he continued.

"But as I went closer to my chair I tried to touch the pile only to discover that the most recent litter was on top with the oldest ones beneath the whole pile. I picked up a bunch of them, threw them into the streets but somehow they came back and remained on my seat. After the third try, I decided to try another tactic. I took all the litter outside town and came back, only to find them multiplied by three and piled up on my favorite chair. By now, my chair was barely visible underneath of trash. Then I decided to put all of them in a trash bag and bring them to the trash shuttle. That's when my favorite chair did not magnetize trash but remained free of it. Then I was mortified, pinched myself to make sure I wasn't dreaming. That was when I saw that many people were going through the same thing as me.", one added. It seemed that everybody has ensued talking at the same time so that potentially no one was listening to what the vicious crowd or the other one was saying but I acknowledged that I understood something drastic was happening here. From the substantial stories being told by these people, I concluded subtly that these people were the infamous ones causing our streets to be dirty and toxic, flawed and full of garbage. The pressure began.

The streets became clean because the trash followed whoever places them in the street floors and around the prairies. The trash also found their way into the homes of the litters, often reaching these pigs' houses even before they got back into their houses. The garbage re-entered their owner's houses faster than these people could enter into their own houses.

Secondly, I noticed that the litter multiplied in size before returning back to their owners' houses. The first time somebody trashed the street, the trash multiplies itself two times before settling in the perceived culprit's house. The second time offender gets it worse; the trash multiplies three times on a second offense and replicates even more as the offender continues to litter the streets.

Third thing I noticed about this is that the only time these trash stop increasing in number and stay where they were left was when they were placed into a trash bag and put where they rightfully belong like in the trash shuttle or on the curb on trash removal days to avoid incidents.

Fourthly, some of these litterers thought their siblings, relatives or friends were playing pranks on them until they spoke to other litterers or neighbors. So my street and the prairie near it is sparkling. I noticed that even the dog poop left by dog owners who never picked up after their dogs found their way into the dog owner's bed. Yes, I said bed. Thanks to Ciji, the awesome debut of our plan worked in perfect ways.

There were still break out of fights in some areas. This occurred mostly in places where people preferred to fight first and talk later. One of the men actually had a gash to the side of his face when one of the others hit him with a ring in his hand. People tried to help and give him first aid as soon as they saw the bloody face. One of the men thought his neighbor was the one bringing smelly trash into his room and vise versa.

People full of bigot were capricious enough to confront their neighbors about the trash issues, some went into their neighbor's houses to totally annihilate their personal belongings. One proceeded to capsize the other one's huge dining table that had pictures of cute canine embedded on top. Then, we saw one man in his early 20s run towards the neighbors. This braggart started yelling out,

"I am the one that made it all happen, I am on a mission to keep our streets clean. If you love yourselves, you better not litter around here because the litter will definitely come back to you multiplied." I looked at my friends, we all looked at him and shook our heads in unison. Then it came out from our mouths simultaneously as if singing a chorus,

"Who is this man?"

Well, we were not about to stand around and huddle with this impostor. We preferred to remain anonymous as the street quickly became congested with people that had one kind of complaint or another in relation to the new found way of keeping our streets clean. Soon, some of them started to hit the exuberant man who confessed to causing their houses to be cluttered with trash. The climax was reached when some started throwing citrus fruits on the man for his flagrant admission of guilt.

Another man gave him a dirty slap on the face while the other one gave him a blow below the belt at which point the 20- something year old man fell down on his knees spreading his hands over his lower body in an effort to protect himself. Suddenly, I developed pity for this victim. I wondered if the crowd meant to kill him. I turned to Ciji and begged him to do something. After Ciji said,

"He put himself into that snare, all by himself." Then he went on to concur with me that the man needed help or else the next angry neighbor might nail him to pieces. Ciji went around the crowd only once as he muttered something beneath his breath and immediately the crowd left off hitting the guy dispersing in different directions. We went forward and tried to take the victim to safety. By this time, he was laying flat on the ground with a few bruises here and there. We resisted the strong urge to reprimand him for the false claim as we helped him, or rather more accurately, carried him into the safety of his house. He was alert enough to point out his house. We went ahead to notify his mother before leaving him in his room. His mother said,

"This dramatic sequel must have followed a new saga he put out there. I know my son, he is very fond of making false claims that lead him to being used as a punching bag. This is not the first time but I hope he learned his lesson". As we headed towards the door, she added, "Thank you so much for bringing him back to me, he better stop because I fear that one of these days, he may not be lucky enough to be rescued in time. This noisome behavior of his not only caused a feud between my family and the neighbors. It had me wondering what species my son came from and if my neighbor's beating of my son is kind of predatory".

As we left him in the safe hands of his mother, I wondered if he did what he did just to gratify his need to be recognized and acclaimed by others but who am I to give the final conclusion on matters like this? All I know was that I felt this warmness in my heart as I noticed once more that our street were as clean as ever. I couldn't prevent the strong urge to high five my friends and I went ahead and did exactly that.

"Kudos, Ciji, kudos", I said. As we walked into the radiant street, I felt so happy that we did help the environment the way we did.

Chapter 13

OBI'S STORY

One cool Saturday afternoon, I was having lunch with my family on our porch when I looked up to see Chima hurrying up the path to my house. A dog, I didn't recognize was close to his heel as he kept coming. I got up instinctively so I could find out what the matter was with him so I asked Chima as he reached my house.

"What is the matter, you look scared to death." The dog that was behind him stood by his side and wagged his brown tail. Chima then told me,

"This is Taja, my new dog."

At which time, Taja started barking at the bag that Chima has in his hand. So I looked at Chima's bag wondering what he got there that was making the dog bark uncontrollably. Whatever he has in this bag was the reason his dog ran behind him to my house and I hoped it wasn't a dead squirrel, or a dead frog. Chima has carried stuff like that in his bag before and I didn't find it funny or entertaining as he did. Personally, I think you can only carry live animals in your bag, as pets maybe but dead ones! No, dead animals should either be buried or left alone if they died in the bush.

Chima took me to the side and whispered,

"I think you need to see this."

Then he opened the bag and at first glimpse I saw a round mirror that resembled one that I saw elsewhere. So I asked him,

"Is that the mirror from…?"

I couldn't finish the question for deep fear and a lump that suddenly came up my throat. It is a scary thing happening here if this mirror is the one I think it looks like, but if it was, then how did it get here like this? What is Chima up to wielding this kind of mirror in his hand like this?

The consequences could be dire if this is "the mirror". Chima nodded vigorously without saying a word, and proceeded to throw up by the side of my house. By now, he looked feverish; he was shaking; there were tears welling up in his eyes. His dog stood transfixed to a spot as soon as Chima threw up. Also the dog stopped barking. It was as if he has been struck by lightning from the bag. Chima's dog kept looking at his bag with eyes that grew big; his head with his tail standing up straight on end.

Then Chima regained his composure enough to say,

"I stole it today." And I said,

"How? Why? How did you even go there by yourself? How did you know for sure that Ciji's parents were there or that they would not come in while you were still there?" I was amazed by the gut and stupidity of my adventurous friends.

"What do you plan to do with it?" I asked. Then Chima took my left hand in desperation drawing farther away from my family by putting more distance between us and the porch. I took a quick glance at my family and they were still having lunch and conversing with one another. This is one of the things I love about my family, they are never too nosy. They trust me enough to let me talk with my friend that is in trouble.

Chima went into a frantic explanation of how he kept thinking about stealing this mirror ever since he laid eyes on it. And I said,

"What?"

Chima continued.

"So finally, I decided to sneak into Ciji's village today and see if I can get my hands on this beautiful mirror. I think this is most beautiful mirror I ever saw."

"Oh, by the way, you might be interested to know that the basilcynth tree has only two leaves left on it." He shrugged as he talked about the leaves left.

"That means we should minimize our visits to shadowland", I added. Chima nodded and then continued to talk.

"I was thinking about this mirror so much that I had to go get it, I just had to go get it", he replied.

I looked at him and shook my head; I thought to myself, I pity this fool right now.

"So I entered shadowland the way Ciji taught us, placed the basilcynth on my forehead and snuck into Ciji's street. Nothing is new in the streets; nothing is new on Ciji's street. Things were the same way, they've always been except for one thing; too many phretas on the streets. I don't know if it is because it is a Saturday but the street was swarming with them so much so that I had to crawl between their legs most part of the way but the street became almost empty again as I neared Ciji's house. I saw only sad-eyed children scattered here and there in Ciji's street. I hastened past them and tiptoed into Ciji's house and listened intently as I quietly went in. Then I did a quick sweep of the place with my eyes before proceeding to pick up the mirror from the floor. As I stretched out my hand to pick it up, I could hear my heart beating uneasily and loudly in my chest. Combined with this was the tick-tock sound of the huge strange clock in Ciji's house. What I saw on the surface of the mirror as I bent it to bevel level made me feel like something pushed my heart into my tummy. For a moment, I froze in my tract as contempt acted on the possibility of a repercussion for taking this mirror. Suddenly, my hunger for this mirror overtook my fear and replaced my emotions with slight uneasiness. And just like that, I snuck out of Ciji's house and Ciji's village safely. Of course, I came with an empty school bag, mine to be precise. I hid the mirror into my school bag as I ran out of Ciji's house. I ran all the way to the end of shadowland where I quickly flew through out of the tree and landed on human side. I breathed a sigh of relief but couldn't stop running until I got to my room. As soon as I reached my room, I became too afraid to look at the mirror all by myself. So I decided to bring it down here so we can play with it together". He finished abruptly.

I was still looking at Chima and trying to decide what to do next. I was looking at Chima and his bag, Taja was looking at Chima and his bag. I could not tell what was going on in the mind of Chima's dog but I bet he was thinking along the same line as me; Chima must be out of his mind to carry out something like this.

"So what do you think will happen when Ciji and his family realize that the mirror is missing?" I asked him.

"Who cares", Chima said.

"All I know is that I felt like taking the mirror and I did." He continued.

I checked the time, it was around twelve noon. So I said,

"Chima, listen. It will be best if you can return this mirror where you found it before they have the capability of finding this mirror and what happens then? They move away from our area and we may never see our friend ever again."

He looked at me briefly and said,

"Look, let's see what this mirror will show us around our town here before we return it, let's play with it for maybe half hour and I will return it if you promise to go with me". I looked around apprehensively as if I expected Ciji and his parents to appear here suddenly before I said,

"You have yourself a deal."

Then almost immediately, I began to regret that I agreed to follow Chima into shadowland today. As I realized what I promised Chima, I took him by the hand and motioned for us to go to his house as we need to leave his dog behind. There's no way we will be able to take Chima's dog to shadowland. Not only would it be impossible to mask the smell of this dog from the ghosts in shadowland. Today is not a good day to try a new thing in shadowland.

As we passed people on the street; as we were taking Chima's dog home; Chima brought out the mirror and we found that some of the people in our village seemed to be floating above the ground whom viewed with this mirror. You can see that these people's feet were not touching the ground. These people were simply gliding past us as if floating by. This is fascinating. All the same, we must hurry up and return "the mirror". While some people's faces showed as monsters through this mirror; other's faces were completely absent when watched through this mirror. It seemed that these last set of people had no heads at all. Then, there were the fourth set of people that didn't appear through this mirror. When the mirror is held against them, the mirror showed just a blank space. None of this made any sense to us but the only person that may be able to explain any of this is the owner of this mirror, Ciji, but he is the last person we would tell about this as the mirror was taken without his permission or knowledge.

As soon as we brought Chima's dog home to Chima's house, we made a dash for Ciji's village. On entering Ciji's village. I kept thinking that we may have forgotten something. Then the unthinkable happened. The ghost dogs that never noticed our presence each time we visited shadowland with Ciji started coming towards us. There were as many as fifty of them and they were slowly making their way towards us; they have a wicked snarl to their faces; their ears all stood up; their tails all stood up straight from behind them as they came towards us. That's when I remembered what it was we forgot to do.

Three words; Basilcynth not applied. I put out my hand, grabbed Chima by his left hand as we turned and ran towards the exit from shadowland. Before stopping in front of the basilcynth, we glanced behind us to see where the ghost dogs were. The emaciated dogs that look half dead were still farther away from us as they were weak and walking towards us instead of running. So, I quickly plucked one leaf of the three leaves left on this weird shrub, rubbed it between my palms to make a pulp and applied it to my forehead and then Chima's just as the ghost dogs were about to bridge the gap between us. We held our breaths as the ghost dogs slowly turned back and walked back to where we found them. That was a close call. I refused to imagine what could have happened if we had been met by ghosts that were in the form of humans or even phretas. By this time, we have already lost thirty minutes of previous time. As we got nearer and nearer to Ciji's house I couldn't stop hoping that nobody would be home. I know I see Chima holding the school bag in his right hand and I also hope the mirror did not fall out on our way here it remained and that intact throughout the travel to here.

As we stepped into Ciji's house, we found it empty of ghosts. I felt happy as we hurriedly removed the mirror from Chima's bag and placed it on the floor near the clock. Then I froze as one look at the mirror showed a tiny crack on the opaque side of it. Then Chima whispered shakily to me "I think the mirror is cracked."

I whispered back,

"I see it."

Then, we quickly ran outside the house only to find that Chima still had the mirror in his right hand. I asked him in a hushed tone, "Why do you still have the mirror?"

And he replied,

"The mirror refused to be placed back, believe me I tried." This brought all sorts of fearful thoughts into my mind. Then I said, "Give it to me."

And I tried to take it from his hand and it seemed like the mirror preferred Chima's hand. Then I yanked it out of Chima's hand and he muffled a cry of pain as the mirror came into my hands. I had to use both hands this time. I ran back into Ciji's house and tried to put the mirror back but to no avail. It seemed like the mirror was in my hand to stay. I thought hard for a second and asked Chima to spit on my hands, then I rubbed the spit all over the mirror, this did not work. So I told Chima to please think of something. By now it was about 4pm and I feared that Ciji and his family might be coming home soon. Then Chima said the one word I have started thinking about,

"Basilcynth!"

So I motioned Ciji to cover my hands with his school bag as we ran back towards this shrub. Then I looked down and saw the leaf pulp we already used earlier today. Chima picked it up and placed it between my fingers and the mirror; it worked. It worked! By this time I was sweating like the cover of a boiling pot.

Finally, we ran back to Ciji's house and placed the mirror back in its spot then crept back outside to start on our run out of shadowland. Just as we were about to make the turn into the cocoa tree, Ciji and his family could be seen coming from the other end of another street. We have narrowly missed being caught in their house. The next day in school, Ciji asked me why we cracked the back of his mirror and I was dumbfounded.

Chapter 14

THE BIRD THAT STOLE THE CHILD

Caro's mother speaks out after I got married to my sweetheart. I started seeing strange things happening around me. On my way to the market place, I sometimes felt that someone was watching me. On the way to the stream, it felt like someone was following me. I couldn't tell anyone about this until scarier things started happening to me. I started seeing one particular bird wherever I go. I know it's the same bird because of the size, the look and the color. This bird is black in color with two stripes of blue on each wing. The beak looked like a shiny shade of silver, the same color of the feet. This bird comes to the windowsill of my bedroom whenever I am there by myself. It appears by the kitchen window when I go there to get something or to cook. This bird always shows up in the stream when I go there. It always finds its way to the market place when I am there. At first, this bird just stares at me as if it would say something but holding itself back from talking.

Then one day, I was relaxing by the stream with my feet inside the stream when I heard my name. It was like a woman's voice but slightly small and hoarse. It called out again,

"Miri, Miri."

I turned to check for the person calling my name; I didn't see anybody. On closer check, there was the little bird that has been following me around since my marriage. As soon as my eyes lighted on it, it said,

"I need to introduce myself to you. My name is Tilda, and I am the one you stole her man" Tilda's voice sounded as if she was there to patronize me. Now I am beginning to understand why this bird started appearing immediately after my marriage but is it possible for a man to date a bird? So I said,

"Tell me how that is at all plausible." To which the bird looked at me with disdain before she said, "Of course, I am a woman like you but after he left me to marry you, I learnt how to change into a bird in order to try and get back what belongs to me."

"It's not that hard to do but I figure you will not need the art unless you get cheated out of something that is rightfully yours", the bird continued. I was going to ask this bird if I can call her Tilda but before I could open my mouth, the bird said,

"Yes, you can call me Tilda."

As I said,

"Tilda, can you explain to me some more?" Tilda has flown away. Then I noticed that more people were arriving at the stream. I realized that this bird only appears to me when there was no one else around. So I told myself that I can avoid seeing Tilda by making sure I went to places that have people there and that I travelled around in the company of other people. On the other hand, I really need answers to the questions I have for this blue- tinged black bird. All I

kept thinking about is how a human being can turn into a little bird. Is she trapped in the body of this bird forever or does she turn back and forth from human to bird and from bird to human whenever and wherever she wants? Are there some rules guiding this transforming art? Can she also turn into other animals or other kinds of birds? I have so many unanswered questions but everything about this bird seemed strange to me. This is the reason I did not mention this bird to my husband or any human being. Plus, I am not about to let people think that I became crazy following my marriage to my handsome husband. How many women start seeing a bird wherever they went after marriage, not to mention a talking black bird for that matter. So not only did I keep all these bird encounters to myself but I also secretly prepared to see this bird again. As curiosity got the better of me, I started thinking of places I could go to see this bird again. I tried to rehearse what I can tell this bird. I planned to ask the bird how I can placate it and make it leave me alone. I managed to see this bird on my way to the stream and it jumped from bush to bush on the way to the stream as I walked along the way. At first, it was as if this bird was my pet bird and was walking with me to the stream. So after we said hi to each other, I asked Tilda how I would know whether what she was saying was true or not. Tilda just said matter-of-factly,

"Ask your husband."

"Ask him who Tilda is.", Tilda continued.

I thought about this briefly before going to my next question.

"So what can I do to get you to leave me alone?" I asked.

Tilda quickly replied,

"Nothing, except leave my husband for me."

"But you were not married to him, Tilda", I said in my reasoning tone.

"But we were engaged before you came into the picture", Tilda shot back.

To which I replied with bewilderment that even showed in my voice.

"But I didn't know about this at all!" Tilda then said,

"We were engaged for two months, 2 days, two hours, two minutes and two seconds before he met you and broke up the engagement. He even had the audacity to tell me he was breaking off with me because of you." Tilda sounded so wounded by this that her voice broke. I felt very sorry for her and ended up saying so. I saw actual teardrops falling down the cheek of this bird. It was quite a site. Tilda suddenly disappeared into the bush as quickly as possible for a bird her size and for the rest of the day I kept thinking about how hurt Tilda sounded as she told me her story. I thought she must be nuts to insinuate I took her husband. It is always better to talk to Arie, my husband, after dinner as he relaxed and wind down from the day's work.

This evening, before I asked my husband the Tilda question, I gave him a back rub and brief body massage to relax him further so that he is not all tensed up as I ask my little question about his ex. I went on in spite of how much I loathed to pursue this.

"Who is Tilda?", I asked abruptly after searching up and down in my mind for the correct way to ask this question. Arie became tensed up and still, then he pushed me aside and got up straight. Arie looked at me with slight suspicion in his eyes before saying,

"What is this all about? You have never asked me about my exes before now." I just kept quiet. I tried hard to keep my facial expression. Then he said,

"Tilda used to be my friend who later became my girlfriend and fiancee for sometime. I felt rushed into the engagement; I didn't feel the connection with her like the way I feel connected with you. She didn't feel right in my heart the way you do. I found it hard to understand her most of the time and this is why I broke up with her." Now, Arie's lengthy reply took words out of my mind. I didn't even have one word to utter. I began to worry my head about what to tell Tilda next time I see her. How possible will it be for me to avoid this little black bird? Maybe I need to encourage my husband to move to a far, far away country; away from Tilda and her talking black bird. I don't think my husband will agree to move; not for something like an angry black bird. After I found my voice, I urged my husband to see if he can explain his decision (to break up with Tilda) to her mainly because it is clear to me that Tilda was not aware of my husband's views in this matter. I said,

"Arie, I think you need to explain what you just told me to Tilda herself. The way you see it may be different from her own perspective about it."

Arie shrugged. From that day forward, I stopped going to places all by myself. I minimized my solo outings making sure I had somebody with me most of the time. What do you know, who showed up on my bedroom window as my husband went to take a shower? Tilda, of course. It's been almost two months since I last saw her so I was taken aback for a moment but quickly recollected my composure. Tilda said in her notorious and infuriating manner,

"Hi", and I said,

"Hi."

Tilda then said in total apathy,

"I'm assuming that you avoided me on purpose all this time. Why?" I said that I found it very strange and unbecoming for a lady to be seen talking to a bird claimed that I stole her husband. Tilda disappeared into the trees before she could say anything more and I knew that my husband was at the bedroom door. Arie came into the bedroom having finished showering. Then, I didn't see Tilda for another five months. By this time I was pregnant with my first baby. We have planned to name this baby, Janu; whether the baby is male or female. Arie was very happy and excited to be a father. I, on the other hand, is a little uneasy. I wanted to be the best mother ever and I didn't feel too sure that I remember thinking that I could always try my best at this. My mother is certainly strive to be one for my unborn child. I have been able to avoid Tilda for almost another five months and by now, I am heavily pregnant and ready to put to bed.

Today has been very hot and the sweltering heat was scorching everything and everybody. I have taken three showers already and after each one, it gradually got hotter as time passed. Finally, I decided to go to the stream by myself. My husband is at work and I am not about to stay away from the cooling stream all because of a little black bird with blue stripes on each wing. I thought to myself what is the worse thing this bird can do? Talk and talk some more. O please, I am going to the stream to cool off the heat. It is likely to be full of other people that are also in a guest to cool off in the face of this heat wave. I felt perfectly fine as I stepped out into the slug street. There were already beads of sweat on my brow from the hot atmosphere. I increased my pace as I kept thinking of how relaxing it will be to have both my feet in the stream or even better still, to dip my whole body into the cool stream. As I hastened some more, I felt a sharp pain to my abdominal area. This cramp like sharp pain stopped me in my track. The pain eased up very quick and I continued on my way to the stream. Soon the pain returned and this time, it was very intense and I started feeling as if I needed to use the toilet. I didn't know much about what is happening to me as this is my very first baby. So I even found it hard to stand up straight to walk; I had to bend down and hold my abdomen with both hands. Clearing from the side way, I turned into this area stooping all the way there.

I reached the clearing and felt as if I was being watched. That eerie feeling came right back and was confirmed by the appearance of Tilda near the clearing. I would have run as fast as my legs could carry me if I had not been in an excruciating abdominal pain. Tilda told me. She was so intent on making me comfortable with her presence that none of us noticed that there were children coming into the path to the stream and one adult also. Tilda just kept talking calmly to me until I delivered my baby in the prairie beside the clearing. I didn't know how Tilda came by an instrument to cut the umbilical cord. Tilda has transformed into a beautiful young woman right before my eyes. She cut the cord and soon turned back into a black bird. Then she swooped down and picked up my baby with two feet. I watched in awe as she got smaller and smaller as she flew away with my first born baby. Since then, nobody has heard from or seen Tilda again.

My story was collaborated by three children and an adult who were passing by and witnessed the birth and abduction of my beautiful firstborn.

So Caro, as you can see, you become our second baby. Till this day, your father tells people to ask me whenever they asked him about our first baby, he still feels flabbergasted by it all.

After what happened, I started wishing that I had given Tilda, the bird, a lethal blow on my previous encounters with her. I wished I had ruptured her nomadic little brain with something. This was one bird that was addicted to abnormal incessant complaints about my spouse. I winked as I contemplated about the little thief who showed up at whim before stealing my child, I thought of the wrath in her little black eyes that she used as a sorry excuse to impede my joy as a new mom. The thought of her simply inundated my mind as I saw her as a vindictive scorned woman that took it upon herself to legacy of vengeance on the wrong person.

Chapter 15

CONCLUSION

Caro's mom never saw Tilda or the black bird again, she has never seen her first born again but Caro, Chima, Ciji and Obi could swear that they often see one black bird with blue stripe on each wing sitting on a tree or flying in the sky with a smaller bird that has a hue of dark purple to the feathers. They are guessing that the smaller bird must be Caro's abducted older sibling.

As for Ciji, he knew almost everything. He knew that we stole the mirror from his house, his parents were also aware of that but his whole family has one goal and one goal only. According to Ciji their main goal is to do good in such an amount as to free them from the limbo they were living in for hundreds of years. Ciji told us that his family did not see the need to move unless people started making them a spectacle. So Ciji continued to be our friend.

My pastor had many questions for me about what I did in church that led to people leaving the village and not looking back. After I told him the story of the basilcynth shrub, he made it a point to talk to me; all my friends and our parents about things like this. Pastor Chuks made an appointment to see all of us and our parents at the church to clarify matters and get to the bottom of all the confusion brought into the church and the lives of family members.

On the day of the meeting, my father who also grew up with Ciji, made it clear to us that we are not going to the church to expose our good friend, Ciji and his family. We only head to talk to the pastor about the basilcynth and nothing more. Anything we say about the ghosts to the pastor must be said without mentioning Ciji's name. There's no need to be specific. We would hate to cause our friend and his family to move.

We arrived at the church in time and waited in the church auditorium for the others to show up. Soon afterwards, Caro and Chima both came in with their parents. The pastor joined us also. After an opening prayer, he turned to me and asked

"What is this thing I am hearing about ghosts and all?" as he sat down and all of us sat down also. I went ahead and told him about a vague ghost story and how some of the children followed some of the ghosts home. I let him know that the ghosts needed to remain where they currently reside so they requested that people not reveal their secret to the public. My pastor took a deep breath before making his final statement and teaching.

"Brethren, please do not forget that ghosts are demons that took the body of dead people in order to walk around and deceive people into believing that a dead person can still be walking around and doing things as if they go to either heaven or hell. Nothing in between those two. Just remember that."

We all needed in affirmation as the pastor was explaining everything. This pastor has a lot of wisdom. He asked us all one question.

"Who can tell me why all the ghost thing is happening?" We, the children, all were dependent on our parents in more ways than one so we held our breaths as we wanted for them to answer.

Our parents probably know why but decided not to utter a word. If the parents are not raising up their hands to answer this question, why should we, the children, be expected to know the answer. Pastor Chuks kept quiet for a bit looking at everyone present for the answer to his question but as it became clear that no one is attempting to answer the question, he continued to speak, saying,

"Each time someone is dead and buried, it is always a step in the right direction to say a prayer over the grave. It has to be the right prayer at the time of burial to prevent any demon from compromising and putting on the likeness of the dead person in order to corrupt others, walk around and frighten people. Pastor Chuks concluded the meeting by telling us a story about what happened when he was in high school. I will write this down in our pastor's own words. Pastor Chuks continues,

"I was just twelve years old, already in high school and getting ready for my confirmation in my church. Two things worth noting about my church at that time: they are (1) they request that you change your name to one that has a known and good meaning if the name you already go by has no meaning or meant something bad like snake, illness and things like that; (2) they preach the gospel to you and allow you to ask questions about the faith before you go through the confirmation. Being confirmed signifies that you are officially a member of this church and that you totally believe and agree with all the beliefs and goods of the church. In this church, you cannot be confirmed into the church before your twelfth birthday."

Pastor Chuks took a deep breath, looking at our faces and continued. We were intrigued by his story.

"I went to the river to wash my clothes on a Saturday morning. On getting nearer to the stream, I noticed two people standing inside the shallow part of the river and yelling out the name of the river and offering things they call sacrifice to this river.

They threw in things like live cocks, a live goat, and some musical instruments. As they were yelling,

"Ulasi, accept our humble gift!"

"Ulasi, accept our humble gift!"

Then the one that dressed like a voodoo doctor who is male stopped, yelling the woman beside him,

"Stay quiet and see the spirits dance as they rejoice over your gifts."

The woman became quiet and suddenly there appeared on top of the water waves movements as of dancing people moving around on the water surface. It was clearly as if people were dancing on the river except the fact that none of the dancers were visible to the human eye. Pastor Chuks continues,

"As I stood there as if thunderstruck by what is happening right here, I started wondering if there could be any viable explanation to this show of invisible dancers in this river."

"That is why the question I had for my church leaders before my confirmation was about this scary water dance. My church leaders explained to me and the other candidates of confirmation that things like this happen so that people will be led to believe that it is their dead ancestors or water spirits accepting the gifts. My church leaders pointed out that the dance simulation is carried out by demons and nobody else. And that is the only plausible explanation. It finally dawned on me that my pastor is correct. What he said made a lot of sense. There are powers. This man of God consulted our parents before inviting us to the church, then he conjured us to stop associating with the spirits of the deceased and calling them "friends". He further advised us to detach ourselves from those counterfeit powers out there to deceive and devour authentic children of God. He also said that the job of those demons is to afflict and dishearten good people. Pastor Chuks said,

"You need a permanent deliverance from such spirits."

Chima raised up his hand, poised to ask a question that has the potential to extend the meeting further. Pastor Chuks perceived that Chima had his left hand up in the air and sent an abrupt nod his way. Chima stood up and with a grave expression on his face proceeded to give a brief narrative before putting his question out there.

Chima began his oration like; talk in a way to pique the interest of those in this meeting. He began,

"How many people get followed home by a young goat, a kid, on the first day of school?" He looked around as he asked this question and as person after person shrugged, he continued,

"I was followed home from school by a black and white kid on the first day of school. I was new to this school and had no friends then. This goat followed me home and refused to leave. My parents asked around in their orthodox way but nobody claimed to be the owner of this goat. This goat slept beside my bed on the floor every night; it followed me around the house and the whole neighborhood. I had to give this goat a name. I called it Oyi. Oyi became inseparable with me. If I was sitting in the parlor, Oyi would be lying next to my feet. If I was walking around, Oyi would be doing the same close to my legs. When I was happy, she would be jumping up, down and around. When I was sad she became sullen and despondent. When I cried she cried also, yes, this goat cried. My neighbors covet my pet goat and overwhelmed parents with persistent complaints about it. They alleged that Oyi made their toddle peevish by sleeping on his docile toy and agitating it. I knew they made up these stories only because Oyi never left my side at all. My firebrand neighbors said that Oyi clambered into their tree house to confront their cat thereby causing their cat to be distraught. I did not believe one word of it and neither did my parents. All I kept thinking about was Oyi's enthralling show of her prowess in prancing. It was quite a sight to behold. Oh and I forgot to mention that my goat looked up at you when you call her name, she even got up from the floor to come to you when you called her name while leaving the room. That brings me to the actual question I have. How can this goat's behavior be explained? How come Oyi was behaving like a dog?" Chima sat down beside his father with his eyes fixed on the pastor for answers. Pastor Chuks thought for a moment before saying,

"I think this question should go to the veterinarian or specialists in animal behaviours."

Afterwards, Chima confided me that the only reason he asked that question was that he thought the goat was some kind of ghost or something. So I asked him if the goat was just a figment of his imagination and he said no, that eve his parents and neighbors interacted with Oyi.

www.ingramcontent.com/pod-product-compliance
Lightning Source LLC
Chambersburg PA
CBHW042035180726
48295CB00006B/106